THE
ANCIENT FOREST

OUTER
SPACE

EMERALD
GLEN

DEADLY
CREEK

GIANTS' TOWN

THE
STINKY
SWAMPS

GOLDEN
COVE

RICKETY
BRIDGE

For Sue and Duncan, from your little monster
R.F.

For Gemma
C.C.

LADYBIRD BOOKS

Ladybird Books is part of the Penguin Random House group of companies
whose addresses can be found at global.penguinrandomhouse.com.

www.penguin.co.uk   www.puffin.co.uk   www.ladybird.co.uk

Penguin
Random House
UK

First published 2018

007

Written by Rhiannon Fielding. Text copyright © Ladybird Books Ltd, 2018
Illustrations copyright © Chris Chatterton, 2018
Moral rights asserted
Printed in China
The authorized representative in the EEA is Penguin Random House Ireland,
Morrison Chambers, 32 Nassau Street, Dublin D02 YH68
A CIP catalogue record for this book is available from the British Library
ISBN: 978–0–241–34891–8
All correspondence to:
Ladybird Books, Penguin Random House Children's
One Embassy Gardens, 8 Viaduct Gardens,
London SW11 7BW

TEN MINUTES TO BED

Little Monster

Rhiannon Fielding · Chris Chatterton

Have you ever **heard** a **monster**
with **horns** upon her head
creeping down the creaky stairs . . .

instead of going to **bed?**

Have you ever seen her
gleaming eyes
or heard her fearsome
growl?

It's
ten minutes
to bedtime,
but someone's
on the
prowl . . .

It's Belch,

the smallest monster,

with a rumbly hairy belly!

It's **nine minutes** to bedtime

and she's downstairs slurping jelly!

Wheeee! Wallop! Whoosh!
Why is there **so much noise?**

It's **eight minutes**
to bedtime . . .
Belch is playing with her **toys!**

In **monster houses**, far and wide,
lie monsters in their beds . . .

so with seven minutes to bedtime,

back down the hall Belch treads.

Squeeeeeak! goes the window.
Dark shadows cross the floor –
it's six minutes to bedtime . . .

but who's bursting
through the door?

It's a herd of little monsters –

it's a sneaky monster ball!

It's five minutes to bedtime . . .

they're not sleepy –
not **at all!**

Cracklebum is upside down

Grouch has caused a riot!

It's four minutes to bedtime
but there's no more
peace and quiet!

Squelch is sliding round on slime,
Gloop's making dreadful smells!
It's three minutes to bedtime . . .

"RIGHT! IT'S TIME FOR BED!"

Belch yells.

Sheepishly, on tired legs,
the others trudge back home.
It's two minutes to bedtime . . .

Belch is pleased to be alone!

Back upstairs and into **bed,**

forgetting to be creepy –

it's **one minute** to bedtime . . .

and she's feeling
warm and sleepy!

See, monsters are a lot **like you**
(except for being **hairy**) . . .

when in their **beds**
they're **sleepyheads** . . .

and not
so very
scary!

THE
ANCIENT FOREST

OUTER
SPACE

EMERALD
GLEN

DEADLY
CREEK

GIANTS' TOWN

THE
STINKY
SWAMPS

GOLDEN
COVE

RICKETY
BRIDGE

Look out for more **bedtime adventures** in

ISBN: 9780241348925 ☐

ISBN: 9780241348918 ✓

ISBN: 9780241372678 ☐

ISBN: 9780241414576 ☐

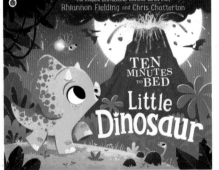

ISBN: 9780241386736 ☐

ISBN: 9780241453162 ☐

ISBN: 9780241464373 ☐